BAD KITTY

Puppy's BIG DAY

NICK BRUEL

SQUARE
FISH

A NEAL PORTER BOOK

ROARING BROOK PRESS

New York

For George and Siobhan: friends and family

SQUARE
FISH

An Imprint of Macmillan
175 Fifth Avenue
New York, NY 10010
mackids.com

Square Fish and the Square Fish logo are trademarks of Macmillan and
are used by Roaring Brook Press under license from Macmillan.

Our books may be purchased in bulk for promotional, educational, or business use.
Please contact your local bookseller or the Macmillan Corporate and Premium
Sales Department at (800) 221-7945 ext. 5442 or by e-mail at
MacmillanSpecialMarkets@macmillan.com.

Library of Congress Cataloging-in-Publication Data

Bruel, Nick, author, illustrator.
Bad Kitty : Puppy's Big Day / Nick Bruel.
       p. cm
   "A Neal Porter Book."
Summary: Uncle Murray takes Puppy on a walk on a day that Bad Kitty is
being unusually difficult, but has several unpleasant encounters with a police
officer and one mean dog along the way. Text is interspersed with information
about dog behavior, pet care, and more.
   ISBN 978-1-250-07330-3 (paperback)
[1. Dogs—Fiction. 2. Cats—Fiction. 3. Humorous Stories.] I. Title.
   PZ7.B82832Badp 2015
[E]—dc23

                                                        2014010357

Special Book Fair Edition ISBN 978-1-62672-307-8
Originally published in the United States by Roaring Brook Press
First Square Fish Edition: 2016
Square Fish logo designed by Filomena Tuosto

            1 3 5 7 9 10 8 6 4 2

AR: 1.0 / LEXILE: 500L

• CONTENTS •

• PART ONE •

PUPPY LAW

In case it's not obvious, Kitty is in a very, very,

VERY

bad mood today.

And nobody knows why.

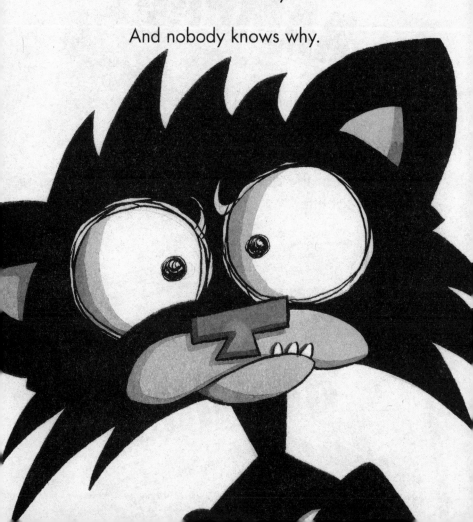

It's worse than the day someone said Kitty needed a bath.

It's worse than the day they discontinued her favorite brand of cat litter.

It's worse than the day they canceled her favorite TV show *Claw and Order*.

THE DAILY NOOZ

MMMM, MMMM . . . NOW THAT'S GOOD NEWS

HORRIBLE RAMPAGE

Hostages were finally released today follow-ing a 5-hour stand off that took place after a local cat lost its mind
Police were

It's even worse than the day we brought Puppy home.

THE DAILY NOOZ

NEWS, NEWS, IT'S GOOD FOR YOUR HEART. THE MORE YOU READ, THE MORE YOU . . .

RAMPAGING HORROR

What is it with this cat?! Just about every month it has some sort of complete melt-
sends every
fleeing

Speaking of Puppy, here he comes now!

Oh, boy. Puppy, if I were you, I'd leave Kitty alone today. I don't think she's in the mood to play with you. Honestly, I don't think she's EVER in the mood to play with you. But today it'll be like playing with a lit firecracker.

Oh, Puppy. Sometimes you just need to listen to reason.

Too late.

HANG ON, PUPPY! I'M CALLING FOR HELP!

15 MINUTES LATER . . .

UNCLE MURRAY IS HERE! I got here as fast as I could! What's the emergency? Are you trying to give that goofy cat a b—?

DON'T SAY IT! DON'T EVEN SAY THE WORD!

15

16

But never mind all that. This ought to be fun! It's been a while since I spent time with a dog. You wanna go to the movies? Or maybe a ball game? Do you know how to play checkers? Maybe we could . . .

Ummm . . . Hello, officer. Good morning to you. Is there anything I can do for you?

YOU GOT A LEASH FOR THAT DOG?

Well, uh, no, officer. Actually, I don't. We were in an awful hurry to leave the house just now, you see, and I guess we forgot it. It's a funny story, actually, if you'd like to hear it. See, there's this goofy cat, and sometimes I'm not even sure if she is a cat. As I was just saying to my dog friend here, sometimes I think . . . and you'll think this is funny . . . sometimes I think she's really a cross between an electric . . .

21

Come on, pooch. Quit your fidgeting! I'm tryin' to get this belt on ya before I get into more trouble.

Say, what ya got there?

23

25

27

Hello again, officer. Lovely day today, isn't it?

YOU GONNA CLEAN UP AFTER THAT DOG?!

Well, officer, do you remember earlier how I was telling you about how I had to leave the house in a big hurry? You remember that, don't you? It was all because of this cat. She can be quite fierce. Really! Anyway, to make a long story short, I left the house so fast that I forgot the leash AND a bag. Silly me! Ordinarily, I would never forget such things. See, I'm quite the advocate of both canine law and sanitation. Why, just the other day my wife was saying to me, "Murray, you should have been a policeman . . .

HOLY SALAMI! This whole dog-walking thing is starting to cost me some big bucks!

32

34

YOU ARE A WISE GUY! HERE'S YOUR TICKET, WISE GUY! NOW GET THAT DOG A LICENSE AND TAKE HIM TO A DOG PARK WHERE OTHER DOGS ARE, WISE GUY!

NO DOGS ALLOWED

The time has come for someone to stand up for dogs' rights in this country! The time has come to reform a system that tickets innocent dog walkers! The time has come to unite all dogs and their walkers and fight the powers that push us down! Someone needs to represent the basic rights and freedoms of all canines and canine perambulators!

41

KITTY'S HORRIBLE BUT TRUE FACTS ABOUT DOGS

Why Do Dogs Need To Be Walked?

This is poop.

This is a time bomb.

Now imagine if some maniac invented a time bomb filled with poop and pee. Someone did. This monstrous combination is known as a dog.

The only way to diffuse this poop bomb from exploding all over your nice clean home and destroying everything you hold dear is by taking it for a walk.

This is not the case for cats.

Cats are delicate, tidy creatures who perform their elimination under controlled conditions. Meaning, they do their business in a litter box out of view.

But not dogs. Dogs need to be walked at least twice a day so that they can relieve themselves anywhere and everywhere they want regardless of the weather outside. It could be raining baseball bats and you'll STILL have to take that dog outside for the privilege of picking up his droppings with a bag. Lucky you.

This is even worse with puppies who need to pee about every 4 hours. That means you'll be walking him 6 times a day or more unless you want to see your stamp collection float away in a river of urine.

Plus, to make things worse, dogs need those walks for exercise because they don't have the insight to sleep 20 hours a day like cats. Most veterinarians say the average dog should be outside for at least 2 hours a day. Good luck with THAT.

STANDARD DOG-WALKING WEATHER

Let's see now ... You had grilled chicken with herbed garden vegetables dog food this morning. Very nice.

You had garlic roasted beef liver for dinner last night But you didn't like that as much. Understandable. Understandable.

Ah, but you managed to steal some scraps of Chinese food takeout last night as well. Shrimp chow fun, I believe. Clever boy!

Your garden grows tulips in the spring and Russian sage ... no ... sorry, sorry ... Mexican sage in the fall.

You live in a three-bedroom ranch style home with a backyard and a porch and a very ornery cat— sorry about that.

No serious allergies. Your blood pressure is normal. You're due for a distemper booster shot. Your favorite color is yellow. You like sunsets, jazz, and long walks in the park. And you're a Capricorn.

So, handsome . . . Now that you and I are boyfriend and girlfriend, I think that you need to give me a lovely little present! Boyfriends always give their girlfriends lovely little presents—beautiful, charming, lovely little presents to express their undying love.

58

65

69

KITTY'S HORRIBLE BUT TRUE FACTS ABOUT DOGS

Why Do Dogs Sniff Butts?

Dogs smell. There are two ways to interpret that sentence. And they're both right.

1. Dogs are smelly. The odor of a wet dog will make you want to rip the nose off your face just to distract you from the pain.

2. Dogs know how to smell. One-third of a dog's brain is dedicated to interpreting smells. (Apparently, the other two-thirds are dedicated to drooling and pooping, but that's a topic for another time.) This means that dogs sense the world around them even more with their noses than they do with their eyes or ears.

A dog's butt gives off a strong odor from an anal gland inside it that can give other dogs a lot of information about it—like what it recently ate, how healthy it is, and even its mood.

So when a dog meets another dog, do they say "Hello. How are you?" No. They can't talk. Do they shake hands? No. They don't have hands. Do they exchange business cards? No. They can't read. Instead, the best way dogs get to know each other is by sniffing each other's butts. Horrible, but true.

Cats, on the other hand, never conduct such behavior. Cats greet each other by licking each other's whiskers, shaking tails, and handing each other formal, handwritten invitations to visit their litter boxes at the earliest convenient opportunity.

Editor's Note: Cats sniff each other's butts, too. They just don't like to talk about it.

Don't you worry, son. You're safe here in the county dog shelter. You get two square meals a day and all the water you can drink. There's a rubber ball around here somewhere to play with, though I ain't seen it in about a year now. And every now and then, an actual beam of sunlight comes through that tiny window up there with the bars. There's nothin' out there in the outside world that can be better than THAT!

Psst. He's crazy.

I should know! I'm **Gramps!** My name is Gramps! But you can call me Gramps. And I've been in here since I was a puppy.

Come to think of it, Gramps is a mighty odd name for a puppy.

But eventually I grew into it. Gramps. I'm Gramps. My name is Gramps.

Freedom tastes like a hot dog that's rolled off the table and under the sofa and now no one wants it because it's all covered in lint and dust. No one, that is, BUT THE DOG!

Freedom tastes like that delicious slice of ham you snatch up when the baby dips it in applesauce and throws it on the floor because the baby just doesn't appreciate fine cuisine.

Freedom tastes like that big, fat mound of tuna fish that's just sitting there all by itself on the counter, and no one is eating it even though it pleads to you, "Eat me, I beg of you, eat me!" So, the only humane thing to do is to jump up there and eat the tuna fish to put it out of its misery because no one else will do it!

I WANT MY TUNA! I WANT MY HAM! I WANT MY LINT-ENCRUSTED HOT DOG! I WANT MY DELICIOUS, DELICIOUS FREEDOM! AND I SHALL HAVE MY FREEDOM, FOR I AM **HERCULES** AND I HAVE A FOOLPROOF PLAN FOR ESCAPE!

You frighten me.

HERCULES' FOOLPROOF

1. COLLECT NAIL CLIPPINGS FROM DOGS.

2. PLACE NAIL CLIPPINGS INTO WAFFLE IRON.

3. REMOVE DELICIOUS-LOOKING (BUT PROBABLY INEDIBL WAFFLE MADE OU OF FUSED DOG NAILS

4. HOLD WAFFLE IN FRONT OF DOGS—CAUSING THEM TO DROOL.

PLAN FOR ESCAPE #591

⑤ COLLECT DROOL IN BOWL.

⑥ HEAT BOWL ON PORTABLE STOVE UNTIL DROOL BOILS.

⑦ CLOUD OF STEAM WILL ALERT GUARD.

⑧ WHEN GUARD ENTERS CAGE TO INVESTIGATE, DOGS SNEAK AWAY UNSEEN IN DROOL STEAM.

⑨ FREEDOM!

Hey there, young fella! Why so glum? You're young. You're good lookin'. I'd say that you stand a pretty good chance of getting adopted and going home with a nice family.

The rest of us . . . well . . . that's a different story.

PLAN FOR ESCAPE #592

5 PLACE FUR INTO MACHINE THAT TURNS DOG HAIR INTO CHEESE.

HAIR

CHEESE

PLACE SETTING ON "BRIE."

6 USE CHEESE TO APPLY FEATHERS TO DOGS.

7 FREEDOM!

WOWEE!

I ran away from my owners. They were not very good dog owners. They treated me very badly, so I ran away. I lived in the dog park up until today.

I don't like to talk about it.

You've got a little microchip just under your skin in the back of your neck that told the shelter who you are and where you live! I bet you didn't even know it was there!

Told ya.

Well, I'll be . . . !

Microchips! Of course! I wish I thought of it!

119

Hi, dog.

I don't think you like me very much. And you probably trust me even less. But that's because you don't know me. See, I'm a nice guy. Really. I don't smoke. I don't gamble. I don't curse . . . well . . . not that often. I have friends. I have a wife who loves me. I have a nice car. I have a nice house with a big backyard. I have a TV with more channels than I can count. I have a lawn mower. I have a refrigerator. I have a blender. I have a machine that can make coffee almost all by itself.

It's kind of incredible, really, when you think about it. All I have to do every morning is pour in a little coffee, pour in a little water, push a button, and five minutes later I have some pretty good coffee. Of course, I have to add in the milk and sugar myself, but . . .

Sorry. I kind of lost track there. What was my point? RIGHT. My point is this—I have lots and lots of stuff. Honestly, I didn't even mention most of the stuff I have.

But the one thing I don't have . . .

126

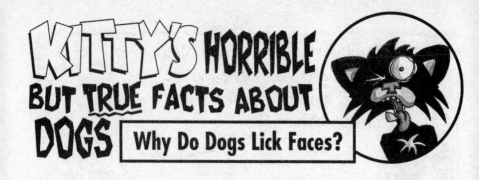

KITTY'S HORRIBLE BUT TRUE FACTS ABOUT DOGS

Why Do Dogs Lick Faces?

Cats rarely lick faces, but when they do it's for the same reasons they lick themselves or other cats: to groom you or taste something that might be interesting. Dogs, however, are different. Very different.

GROSS.
DO NOT TOUCH
KEEP AWAY

Dogs lick people because they're hoping to eat any regurgitated food you might have on your face. THAT'S RIGHT! YOU READ THAT RIGHT! DON'T TURN AWAY! FACE THE UGLY TRUTH! Dogs want to eat your throw up!

Say a wild dog, like a wolf mother, kills a deer. Rather than try to drag her prey all the way back to her den, she'll eat as much as she can and then carry her food back inside her stomach. Her puppies will then lick her face to make her regurgitate her food for them to eat. And if this notion doesn't make you want to regurgitate your own breakfast, then I don't know what else will.

This means that when a dog or a puppy licks YOUR face, he's following the same instinct he used when he wanted his mother to vomit on him. I REPEAT . . . Puppies WANT their mothers to vomit on them.

CARTOON BY KITTY

Oh sure, dogs will lick people's faces for other reasons. They like the taste of your salty sweat and tears. They might like the taste of that new skin lotion you're using.

And, of course, dogs like to lick people as a sign of affection or excitement or happiness. Dogs sometimes lick people's faces as a sign of submission just as they once did with their own mothers. Licking is a signal they give to people that they're comfortable around you.

But regardless of the reasons, licking people is gross. Dogs are gross. And licking people is just another item in a long list of disgusting dog habits.

So if there are any cats out there reading this who actually lick people—that is a sick dog thing. SO CUT IT OUT!

*If you LICK, you are SICK!

• PART FOUR •

PUPPY LOYALTY

141

143

WELCOME HOME, PUPPY! Boy, we're glad to have you back safe and sound. But we have to warn you— Kitty is still just as ornery and cross as ever, and we still can't figure out why.

I've been busy digging an underground bunker in the backyard where we can all live from now on.

Puppy, did you hear me? Approaching Kitty right now is probably a terrible idea.

Puppy? Puppy? Uh-oh.

Puppy! You found Mousey-mouse! I haven't seen Mousey-mouse since yesterday.

Wait a minute . . .

All this mayhem—all this chaos—all of this wanton carnage and destruction—this is all because Mousey-mouse was missing?

ARE YOU KIDDING ME?!

KITTY, IS THIS WHY YOU'VE BEEN IN SUCH A FOUL, WRETCHED MOOD ALL DAY? IS THIS WHY WE'VE BEEN LIVING IN CONSTANT TERROR ALL THIS TIME? IS THIS WHY THE PIANO IS ON THE ROOF AND THE CAR IS IN THE BASE-MENT? IS THIS WHY OUR NEIGHBORS HAVE CHANGED THEIR NAMES AND MOVED OUT OF THE COUNTRY? ALL THIS—ALL THIS BECAUSE YOU COULDN'T FIND MOUSEY-MOUSE FOR ONE STINK-ING DAY?! IS THIS SOME KIND OF SICK JOKE? KITTY! KITTY! DON'T YOU DARE IGNORE ME. KITTY THIS IS SERIOUS! KITTY, I KNOW YOU CAN HEAR ME! KITTY, WE HAVE TO HAVE A VERY SERIOUS ALL THIS!

MEET THE BREEDS

Petunia • Bulldog

Despite its stern and formidable appearance, the bulldog is a very loving and gentle pet. But they did once have a very savage side to their personality when they were first bred to leap up and bite a bull's nose with their powerful jaws just before bullfights. But this ferocious past is long behind them.

Hercules • Chihuahua

Though considered the smallest dogs in the world and weighing as little as only 2 pounds, chihuahuas can have a fierce and dominating personality. Archaeologists have discovered the remains of these dogs inside of Mayan tombs, because people believed them to be so sacred that they could guide them in the afterlife.

Gramps • Lhasa Apso

The history of these dogs goes back more than 1,300 years to when they were guard dogs in Tibetan monasteries. Though their eyesight is compromised by the long hair that covers their faces, their hearing is exceptionally good. As you can imagine, that luxurious coat of theirs requires daily brushing to stay that way.

Puppy • Mutt

Any dog whose breed cannot be recognized, usually because it's a blend of two or more breeds, is commonly known as a "mutt" or "mongrel." These dogs are just as loving and fun as any purebred. In fact, studies have shown that mutts tend to be healthier and live longer than their purebred cousins.

PET ADOPTION

There are an estimated 6 MILLION to 8 MILLION dogs and cats living in pet shelters in the United States. Only about 25 percent of them are ever adopted. Although these shelters do their absolute best to keep their animals healthy and safe, the reality is that they are all overcrowded.

For information on how you can help animals living in shelters go to . . .

humanesociety.org
or
aspca.org

For information on how you can find the right pet for you to adopt from a shelter go to . . .

adoptapet.com
or
petfinder.com

More BAD🐾KITTY Madness!

Dear Nick Bruel,

Thank you for finishing these sentences.

XO,

SQUARE FISH

If I were a puppy . . .

then I would do everything in my power to enjoy being a puppy. I was a puppy once. I used to frolic outside and run around the house and roll in dirt without a care in the world. I used to play with such enthusiasm that I thought I would never tire out. But then I grew up and became a big, tired, old dog. And now that I am an old dog, I have come to realize that I never really appreciated how wonderful it was to be a puppy. And now, of course, I miss it. Being an old dog isn't that bad. But being a puppy was better.

I always . . .

read to my puppy every night. Our daughter Izzy can't fall asleep without having at least two books read to her every night. And in case anyone is wondering, her favorite books are NOT Bad Kitty books. She loves books by Ezra Jack Keats and Cynthia Rylant and Arnold Lobel. So do I.

I wish I could . . .

play the piano and speak Chinese. These, of course, were the two things my mother wanted me to do the most, but I was very resistant when I was a puppy. And now I regret it. I am comforted, however, by the notion that it's never too late. The only question, though, is whether or not an old dog can learn new tricks.

Puppy should . . .

do whatever he can to make that cat play with him. He will always fail, but he should never give up.

Puppy loves . . .

to play. PLAY! PLAY! PLAY!

Kitty loves . . .

to sleep. SLEEP! SLEEP! SLEEP! This is one reason why Kitty and Puppy have trouble finding common ground.

When I'm in a bad mood . . .

I try to take a shower. Long, hot showers clear my head better than anything else. Not coincidentally, perhaps, a long shower is also often the source of great creative inspiration for me.

Look! It's a . . .

massive, powdery white ice crystal beast floating in the sky! **Where?!** There! **Where?!** Right in front of you! **Where?!** Right there above us! **You mean that thing?!** It's about to drop on us and crush us all like a bowling ball rolling over an anthill! **You mean that?!** YES, THAT! **That's a cloud.** A what? **A cloud.** Oh . . . then maybe we should get an umbrella.

But why didn't you ask me about . . .

my recipe for baked salmon? Mix together 1/4 cup of lemon and/or lime juice with 1/4 cup of olive oil and two finely chopped cloves of garlic. Pour the mixture over a large filet of salmon lying skin side down on aluminum foil. Wrap the foil loosely around the fish and seal up the top. Marinate the fish in the refrigerator for an hour or longer. Bake at 375 degrees Fahrenheit for about 30 minutes. Delicious.

Editor's note: Kids, remember not to use the oven yourself! If you want some salmon, give this recipe to a responsible adult.